Christmas in Kentucky

KAYLA LOWE

Want a free book? Sign up to my newsletter to get my award-winning book for free! www.authorkaylalowe.com

<h1 style="text-align:center">More of My Books</h1>

Series

Christmas Blessings

Christmas Miracle for Two
A Christmas Promise of Love
A Christmas of Renewed Faith

Women of the Bible Fiction

Ruth
Esther
Rachel
Hannah
Deborah

❄

Charms of the Chaste Court

A Courtship in Covent Garden
Whispers in Westminster
Romance in Regent's Park
Serenade on Strand Street
Treasure in Tower Bridge

<u>Sweet Honey by the Sea</u>

<u>The Beekeeper's Secret (Book 1)</u>
<u>A Royal Honeycomb (Book 2)</u>
<u>Bees in Blossom (Book 3)</u>
<u>Honeyed Kisses (Book 4)</u>
<u>Blooming Forever (Book 5)</u>

<u>Strawberry Beach Series</u>

<u>Beachside Lessons (Book 1)</u>
<u>Beachside Lessons (Book 2)</u>
<u>Beachside Lessons (Book 3)</u>

Panama City Beach Series

Sun-Kissed Secrets (Book 1)
Sun-Kissed Secrets (Book 2)
Sun-Kissed Secrets (Book 3)

The Tainted Love Saga

Of Love and Deception (Book 1)
Of Love and Family (Book 2)
Of Love and Violence (Book 3)

Of Love and Abuse(Book 4)
Of Love and Crime (Book 5)
Of Love and Addiction (Book 6)
Of Love and Redemption (Book 7)

Standalones

Maiden's Blush

Poetry

Phantom Poetry
Lost and Found

Chapter One

Courtney Rivera's heels clicked against the weathered wood of her grandmother's front porch. As she fumbled for the key, her gaze settled on the faded rocking chair where her grandmother had spent countless evenings spinning tales and sharing life lessons. A lump formed in Courtney's throat as she pushed open the door.

Inside, the familiar scent of cinnamon and vanilla wrapped around her like a warm hug. Courtney set down her designer suitcase, taking in the cozy living room with its crocheted afghans and framed family photos. Memories flooded back—summers spent chasing fireflies, winters curled up by the hearth listening to Aunt her grandmother's soothing voice recite Bible verses.

"Oh Grandma," Courtney whispered, a tear sliding down her cheek. "I miss you so much already."

She wandered into the kitchen, trailing her fingers along the countertop. In her mind's eye, she could see her grandmother, apron tied snugly around her waist, humming hymns as she rolled out dough for apple pies. The ache in Courtney's chest intensified.

"Why did I stay away so long?" she murmured, guilt tugging at her heartstrings. The fast pace of city life had consumed her, leaving little time for visits home. Now, standing amidst the remnants of her grandmother's love, Courtney yearned for the simplicity and comfort of her childhood.

With a sigh, she opened the fridge, smiling wistfully at the containers of her grandmother's famous chicken and dumplings. Courtney knew each dish was prepared with a prayer and a sprinkle of faith. She grabbed a Tupperware, suddenly ravenous for a taste of home.

As she sat at the worn wooden table, savoring each bite, Courtney's mind drifted to simpler times —lazy afternoons shelling peas on the porch swing, giggling with her grandmother over glasses of sweet tea. A pang of longing pierced her heart.

"I don't know if I'm cut out for the corporate world anymore," she admitted aloud, her voice echoing in the empty kitchen. "My soul feels so weary, Grandma. What would you tell me to do?"

In the silence, Courtney could almost hear her grandmother's gentle wisdom: *Listen to your heart, sweet pea. The Lord will guide your path.*

With a deep breath, Courtney cleared her plate and wandered out onto the back porch. The rolling Kentucky hills stretched before her. She inhaled the crisp air, feeling a sense of peace wash over her troubled spirit.

Maybe, just maybe, this trip home would help her rediscover what truly mattered. With a whispered prayer, Courtney surrendered her uncertainties to the One who had always been her strength. Her grandmother's love, even from heaven, would light the way.

The crunch of tires on gravel pulled Courtney from her reverie. A familiar old pickup truck rolled to a stop in front of the house, its faded blue paint a testament to years of hard work. The driver's door swung open, and a tall figure emerged, his broad shoulders stretching a well-worn flannel shirt.

"Tony Turner, as I live and breathe," Courtney called out, a smile tugging at her lips. She stepped off the porch, memories of childhood adventures flooding her mind.

"Well, if it isn't Courtney Rivera, the big-city hotshot," Tony teased, his blue eyes crinkling at the corners. He strode over, enveloping her in a warm hug that smelled of earth and sunshine. "Welcome home, Court."

Courtney melted into the embrace, surprised by the sudden rush of emotions. "It's good to be back," she murmured, blinking away the sting of tears. "I just wish it were under better circumstances."

Tony pulled back, his calloused hands resting gently on her shoulders. "I'm so sorry about your grandma, Courtney. She was a special lady."

"She sure was," Courtney agreed, her voice catching. She cleared her throat, desperate to change the subject. "So, what brings you out this way?"

"Oh, you know, just helping the Johnsons with their post-harvest clean-up," Tony shrugged, his gaze drifting to the fields beyond. "It's been a long season, but we're all pitching in to get things squared away before winter hits."

Courtney nodded, a pang of guilt niggling at her heart. Here she was, worrying about her own problems, while her childhood friend spent his days serving others. "That's really kind of you, Tony. I'm sure they appreciate the help."

"Ah, it's nothing," he waved off the praise, a hint of a blush creeping up his neck. "Just doing what needs to be done. That's the way it is around here."

An awkward silence stretched between them, the weight of years apart suddenly palpable. Courtney scuffed the toe of her designer boot against the gravel, searching for the right words.

"So, how's life in the big city treating you?" Tony finally asked, his tone light but his eyes searching. "I bet it's a far cry from this little old town."

Courtney laughed, a brittle sound even to her own ears. "Oh, you know, it's...it's something else. Always busy, always rushing. Sometimes I wonder if I'm really living, or just existing."

The words hung heavy in the air, an admission she hadn't even made to herself. Tony studied her face, his expression softening with understanding.

"I know what you mean," he said quietly, his gaze drifting to the horizon. "There are days when I wonder if I'm doing the right thing, staying here on the farm. If maybe I should've followed a different path, like you did."

Courtney's heart clenched at the wistfulness in his voice. She reached out, her hand finding his, rough and warm. "You're doing important work here, Tony. This community needs people like you, with roots that run deep and a heart that gives endlessly."

He smiled then, a genuine, lopsided grin that transported Courtney back to summers spent chasing fireflies and whispering secrets in the hayloft. "And the world needs people like you, Courtney. People who dream big and chase their passions, no matter where they lead."

They stood there, hands clasped, as the golden light of late afternoon bathed the farmyard in a gentle glow. For a moment, the years melted away, and Courtney felt a flicker of something long-forgotten stir in her soul.

Chapter Two

Courtney gazed out the window of her grandmother's cozy living room, her eyes tracing the familiar contours of the rolling hills and patchwork fields that stretched to the horizon. The sun hung low in the sky, painting the landscape in hues of amber and gold, a breathtaking tableau that tugged at her heartstrings.

She sighed, her thoughts drifting to the towering skyscrapers and bustling streets of the city she now called home. The constant hum of activity, the endless meetings, and the relentless pursuit of success had become her life's rhythm, but here, in the quiet solitude of her hometown, she found herself questioning if that rhythm truly resonated with her soul.

Courtney's hand reached for the worn photo

album on the coffee table, its pages filled with memories of a simpler time. She traced her fingers over the images of her younger self, laughing with Tony as they raced through the fields, their cares as light as the summer breeze. A smile played at the corners of her lips, tinged with a bittersweet longing for the innocence and joy of those carefree days.

The weight of her grandmother's passing, combined with the unexpected reconnection with Tony, had stirred a deep well of emotions within her. The city life had given her success, but at what cost? Had she sacrificed the chance for true happiness, for a life rooted in the love and warmth of family and community?

Courtney's gaze drifted to the family photos that adorned the walls, generations of Riveras smiling back at her. She felt a sudden yearning to be part of something bigger than herself, to build a life that honored the legacy of love and resilience that had shaped her.

She picked up a photo album and opened it, nostalgia washing over.

As she turned the pages of the photo album, Courtney's vision blurred with unshed tears. Each snapshot was a window into a cherished past, a testament to the love and laughter that had filled her grandmother's home. The images of Courtney and her grandmother, their faces alight with joy as they baked cookies, tended to the garden, and sang hymns on the front porch, pierced her heart with a bitter-sweet ache.

Memories flooded Courtney's mind, vivid and visceral. She could almost smell the fragrant aroma of her grandmother's signature apple pie wafting from the kitchen, could almost feel the warmth of her embrace as they snuggled under a handmade quilt, could almost hear the sweet cadence of her voice as she recited passages of Scripture. Each recollection was a precious gem, a glittering facet of the love that had shaped Courtney's life.

But amidst the nostalgia, a sharp pang of guilt twisted in Courtney's chest. The pages of the album were a stark reminder of the moments she had missed, the opportunities to create new memories that she had allowed to slip away. The demands of her fast-paced city life had consumed her, leaving little room for the quiet moments and heartfelt conversations that her grandmother had always cherished.

Tears began to spill down Courtney's cheeks, hot and heavy with regret. She thought of all the phone calls cut short, the visits postponed, the holidays spent apart. She had always assumed there would be more time, more chances to sit at her grandmother's feet and soak in her wisdom, to bask in the unconditional love that radiated from her very being.

Now, as she sat surrounded by the remnants of her grandmother's life, Courtney felt the weight of those lost moments pressing down upon her. The ticking of the antique clock on the mantel seemed to echo the passage of time, each second a reminder of the precious memories that could never be reclaimed.

Courtney closed the album, her fingers trembling as she traced the worn leather cover. She drew in a shuddering breath, the scent of her grandmother's perfume still lingering in the air, a ghostly presence that only amplified the ache in her heart.

"I'm so sorry, Grandma," she whispered, her voice cracking under the weight of her emotions. "I should have been here more. I should have made the time. I just...I got so caught up in my own life, in chasing my dreams, that I forgot what truly mattered."

The tears flowed freely now, a cleansing stream that washed away the veneer of composure Courtney had so carefully constructed. She wept for the laughter unshared, for the stories untold, for the love that had always been her guiding light.

As the sobs wracked her body, Courtney felt a gentle warmth envelop her, like the comforting embrace of her grandmother's love. It was a sensation she hadn't felt in far too long, a balm to her weary soul. She closed her eyes, allowing herself to be cradled by the memories, by the unshakable faith that had been her grandmother's greatest gift.

In the stillness of the moment, Courtney could almost hear her grandmother's voice, soft and tender, whispering words of reassurance.

But she didn't feel like she deserved them.

Chapter Three

The bell above the diner door jingled as Courtney stepped inside, a gust of frigid air swirling in behind her. She shrugged off her coat, her eyes taking in the cozy interior—the checkered floor, the aroma of fresh coffee and frying bacon, the gentle murmur of conversation from the handful of patrons.

She remembered having many a breakfast here with her grandma.

She slid into a booth, the red vinyl seat creaking beneath her. A plump, rosy-cheeked waitress bustled over, pen poised over her order pad. "What can I getcha, hon?"

"Coffee, please. And a slice of that cherry pie I see

in the display case." Courtney smiled. Gran had always loved this diner's cherry pie. The memory brought a lump to her throat.

As the waitress hurried off, the bell jingled again. Courtney glanced up to see a familiar figure stomping snow from his boots. Beneath a bearded face reddened by the cold, kind eyes met hers.

Tony.

"Courtney." He ambled over, a warm smile spreading across his face. "Fancy runnin' into you here."

She laughed. "It's good to see you too, Tony. Please, have a seat."

He slid into the booth across from her, shrugging out of his coat. "How you holdin' up?"

Courtney traced a finger along the diner mug the waitress set in front of her. "I'm...managing. It's harder being back in Gran's house than I thought it would be, with all the memories."

Tony nodded, his eyes soft with understanding. "I reckon it ain't easy. But you know, times like these, it helps to lean on faith and community. In fact..." He hesitated, then continued. "There's a real nice service at the church this Sunday. Candle-lighting, carols, the works. I'd be honored if you'd come with me."

Courtney bit her lip. It had been a long time since she'd set foot in a church. But the idea of being surrounded by the warmth of the congregation, of reconnecting with her roots...it held an undeniable appeal.

She met Tony's earnest gaze and found herself nodding. "I'd like that. Thank you, Tony."

His smile could have melted the snow outside. "Wonderful. I'll pick you up at ten on Sunday." He reached across the table and squeezed her hand. "You're not alone in this, Courtney. Remember that. A lot of people here loved Miss Helen."

As she squeezed his hand back, Courtney felt something kindle in her heart that had long been dormant.

Hope.

And for the first time since Gran's passing, the idea of staying in Kentucky a little longer didn't seem so daunting after all.

The rich harmonies of the church choir washed over Courtney as she sat beside Tony in the old wooden pew. Sunlight streamed through the stained glass windows, casting a kaleidoscope of colors across the congregation. The scent of fresh evergreen wreaths mingled with the warm aroma of beeswax candles, enveloping her in a comforting embrace.

As the reverend spoke of hope, faith, and the enduring love of family, Courtney felt her throat tighten with emotion. She glanced around at the faces of the churchgoers—some familiar from her childhood, others new but no less welcoming. In their smiles and nods of acknowledgment, she felt a sense of belonging that had eluded her for years in the fast-paced world of the city.

Tony's deep baritone joined the chorus of "Silent Night," and Courtney found herself singing along, the words flowing from a place of long-forgotten memory. As the final notes faded away, she felt a peace settle over her, a quiet assurance that she was exactly where she needed to be.

After the service, Courtney and Tony walked hand in hand back to Gran's house, their breath frosting in the crisp winter air. As they stepped inside, Courtney was struck by a sudden desire to explore more of her grandmother's life.

"I think I'm going to look through some of Gran's things," she said, shrugging off her coat. "I feel like there's so much about her I still don't know."

Tony smiled, his eyes warm with understanding.

"You take all the time you need. I'll put on some coffee."

Courtney climbed the stairs to Gran's bedroom, her fingers trailing along the familiar banister. She pushed open the door and stood for a moment, taking in the quilt-covered bed, the antique dresser, the rocking chair by the window where Gran had spent countless hours knitting and reading her Bible.

On the nightstand sat a worn leather journal, its pages edged in gold. Courtney picked it up, running her fingers over the soft cover. She settled into the rocking chair and opened the journal, her grandmother's elegant script flowing across the pages.

As she read, Courtney felt as though Gran were there beside her, sharing her wisdom and her unwavering faith. Stories of love, loss, and the resilience of the human spirit filled the pages, each one a testament to the remarkable woman her grandmother had been.

Tears blurred her vision as she read the final entry, penned just days before Gran's passing:

My dearest Courtney, know that wherever life takes you, you will always have the strength of our family, the love of

our Lord, and the memories of this place
to guide you home.

Courtney hugged the journal to her chest, a smile tugging at her lips even as tears tracked down her cheeks. For the first time in years, she felt truly connected to her roots, to her grandmother's legacy.

She closed her eyes, breathing in the scent of Gran's perfume that still clung to the room. Outside, the church bells began to ring, their peals echoing across the snow-covered hills of Kentucky like a promise of hope and new beginnings.

Courtney stepped out onto the porch, the cold winter air a sharp contrast to the warmth that had enveloped her moments before. She tucked Gran's journal into her coat, a physical reminder of the connection she'd just rediscovered.

The sun hung low on the horizon, casting a golden glow across the snow-dusted fields. In the distance, she could see the steeple of the church where she'd found solace earlier that day. The sight brought a smile to her face, though a moment later her heart panged with sadness at the thought that she'd never sit in the pew with her grandma again.

"Penny for your thoughts?" a familiar voice spoke next to her. Courtney turned to see Tony. He came out of the house bearing mugs of steaming hot coffee.

"Just taking in the view," Courtney replied as she gratefully took a cup and gestured to the landscape before them. "I never realized how beautiful it was here."

Tony nodded, coming to stand beside her. "It has a way of sneaking up on you, doesn't it? The beauty, the sense of belonging."

Courtney met his gaze, her heart fluttering at the understanding she saw there. "I'm starting to see that. And I'm starting to wonder..." She paused, the words caught in her throat.

"Wonder what?" Tony prompted gently.

"If maybe there's a reason I came back here, beyond just settling Gran's estate. If maybe...maybe I'm meant to stay a while longer."

Tony's smile widened, his eyes crinkling at the corners. "Well, I for one think that sounds like a mighty fine idea. This town could use a woman like you in it, Courtney Rivera."

Courtney laughed, the sound carried away on the winter breeze.

Tony held up a hand and grinned. "All I'm saying is you should at least stay through Christmas. Take some time to grieve and reconnect."

Courtney nodded. "Yes," she agreed, and for the first time in a long time, the future seemed full of possibility, and Kentucky felt less like a place to leave behind and more like a place to call home.

Chapter Four

The bell on the cafe door jingled as Courtney stepped inside, a gust of chilly winter air following her. She unwrapped her scarf and glanced around the cozy interior, spotting Tony waving at her from a corner booth.

"Courtney! Over here," he called out with a warm smile. She navigated through the bustling tables and slid into the seat across from him.

They ordered coffee and settled into easy conversation, swapping stories about their lives since high school. Courtney found herself captivated by the passion in Tony's voice as he described working his family's land. But there was an undercurrent of worry too.

"Honestly, it's been a tough few years," Tony admitted, fidgeting with his mug. "Crop yields are down, and we're struggling to make ends meet. I've been racking my brain trying to figure out how to turn things around."

Courtney's heart ached for him. She knew how much that farm meant to Tony and his family. Seeing the weariness in his normally bright eyes, an idea began to take shape.

"Have you considered updating your marketing strategy?" she asked gently. "With the right campaign, you could expand your customer base, maybe even partner with local businesses. I'd be happy to help brainstorm some ideas, put together a plan."

Tony's eyes widened. "You'd do that? Courtney, that would be amazing. I can't thank you enough."

She reached over to pat his arm. "That's what friends are for. We'll figure this out together, I promise."

As they huddled over the table, sketching out ideas on napkins, Courtney felt a long-forgotten warmth bloom in her chest.

It felt good to be helping someone.

The sun hung low in the sky as Courtney and Tony walked side by side through the rows of his family's farm. The rich, earthy scent of freshly tilled soil filled the air, mingling with the sweet aroma of ripening produce. Tony knelt down, plucking a perfectly ripe tomato from the vine.

"Remember when we used to sneak out here as kids?" he asked, a mischievous grin spreading across his face. "We'd 'sample' the crops and thought no one would notice."

Courtney laughed, the sound carrying across the quiet fields. "Your dad caught us red-handed once, literally. We had tomato juice all over our faces."

"He was more amused than angry, though. Told us if we were going to steal his tomatoes, we might as well learn how to pick the best ones."

They continued down the row, their hands brushing occasionally as they reached for the plumpest fruits. Courtney marveled at the care and dedication evident in every plant, each one nurtured by Tony's patient hands.

As they worked, they traded stories of their childhood adventures—the time they got lost in the cornfield, the day they rescued a stray kitten from the barn. Each memory was a thread, weaving their hearts back together.

Tony paused, wiping the sweat from his brow with the back of his hand. "I've missed this," he said softly, his eyes meeting Courtney's. "Missed you."

Courtney's breath caught in her throat. The sincerity in his voice, the tenderness in his gaze—it stirred something deep within her, a longing she thought she had left behind years ago.

"I've missed you too, Tony. More than I realized."

They stood there for a moment, the silence between them filled with unspoken emotions. Then Tony cleared his throat, holding up a basket brimming with ripe vegetables.

"We should get these inside. I've got an apple pie cooling on the windowsill. Thought we could slice it up and chat more about those marketing ideas of yours."

Courtney nodded, a smile tugging at her lips. As they walked back towards the farmhouse, their arms brushing with each step, she couldn't shake the feeling that this—being here with Tony, working towards a shared goal—was exactly what she needed. A sense of purpose, of connection, that she'd been missing for far too long.

And deep down, in a part of her heart she had long tried to ignore, Courtney felt the stirrings of something more. Something warm and bright and full of promise, like the first rays of sun after a long, cold winter.

She peeked a look at Tony and then looked away quickly, her face flushing.

Chapter Five

The festive glow of string lights sparkled throughout the town square as Courtney joined the throng of people gathering for the annual holiday festival. Familiar faces greeted her with warm smiles and friendly waves, everyone bundled up in cozy sweaters and scarves against the crisp winter air. The scent of hot cocoa and cinnamon wafted from the refreshment stand, mingling with the laughter of children playing tag around the central fountain.

"Courtney, is that you?" called out Mrs. Turner, her third grade teacher. The woman's kind eyes crinkled as she beamed at her former pupil. "I haven't seen you in ages! Look at you, all grown up and successful in the big city. We're so proud of you, dear."

Courtney returned the smile and stepped forward to embrace her. "It's wonderful to see you too, Mrs. Turner. This town will always be home to me, no matter where I go."

As she moved through the crowd, Courtney couldn't help but marvel at the effortless camaraderie on display. Neighbors swapped recipes and shared updates on their families, while old friends reminisced about high school shenanigans. A deep sense of belonging filled her heart, reminding Courtney of the unbreakable bonds that tied this community together.

Later that evening, curled up on the couch with a soft throw blanket, Courtney carefully opened her grandmother's worn leather journal. The pages were filled with elegant script, detailing a life of unwavering faith and enduring love. As she read, Courtney could almost hear her grandmother's gentle voice imparting wisdom and encouragement.

One passage in particular caught her eye:

> *In times of doubt or hardship,*
> *remember that God's love is a constant*

light guiding you forward. Trust in His
plan, even when the path seems uncertain.

Tears welled up as Courtney traced the words with her fingertip. She could picture her grandmother, bible in hand. Her faith had been an inspiration to so many. Her grandma's story inspired her, filling Courtney with a renewed sense of hope and purpose.

With a soft smile, she hugged the journal close to her heart, feeling the warmth of her grandmother's love enveloping her like a comforting embrace.

The shrill ring of her phone jolted Courtney from her reflections. She reached for it, her heart skipping a beat when she saw Tony's name on the screen. With a deep breath, she answered, "Hey there, stranger."

Tony's warm chuckle filled her ear. "Hey yourself, city girl. I was hoping you might be free for dinner tonight. Mom and Dad have been asking about you non-stop since they heard you were back in town."

Courtney felt a flutter of nervousness mixed with excitement. "Dinner with the Turners? How could I possibly refuse?"

"Great! Come on over to the farm around 6.

Mom's making her famous pot roast, and I promise Dad won't break out the embarrassing childhood photos...at least not right away."

She laughed, the sound genuine and carefree. "I'll be there with bells on. And I'll hold you to that promise about the photos!"

As the call ended, Courtney found herself grinning from ear to ear. The prospect of an evening with Tony and his parents, surrounded by the warmth and love of their family, filled her with a joy she hadn't felt in years.

Chapter Six

The sun was just beginning to dip below the horizon when Courtney pulled up to the Turner family farm. The white farmhouse stood proud amidst the sprawling fields, its porch lined with rocking chairs and potted geraniums. Memories of summers spent chasing fireflies and sipping lemonade on that very porch flooded her mind as she approached the front door.

Before she could even knock, the door swung open, revealing Mr. Turner's beaming face. "There she is! Get on in here, Courtney."

He pulled her into a hug, the scent of hay and sunshine clinging to his flannel shirt. Courtney melted into the embrace, feeling a sense of coming home wash over her.

"James, is that Courtney?" a warm, maternal voice called from the kitchen.

"Sure is, Eileen!" James replied, ushering Courtney inside.

Stepping into the farmhouse was like stepping back in time. The living room was adorned with handmade quilts and family photos, the air perfumed with the mouthwatering aroma of pot roast and freshly baked bread.

Eileen, emerged from the kitchen, her face alight with joy. She immediately enveloped Courtney in a motherly hug, whispering, "Welcome home, sweetheart."

James, his eyes crinkling with mirth, chimed in, "Looks like our little troublemaker is all grown up!"

Just then Tony walked in, grinning ear to ear as he saw the warm reception his parents were giving Courtney. "Hope they're not smothering you too much, Court."

Courtney laughed, the sound mingling with the clinking of dishes as they settled around the dining table. "No, it's great to see you all too."

Stories began to flow, tales of childhood mischief and teenage hijinks.

"Remember when you two decided to 'paint' the barn using mud after that big rainstorm?" Eileen reminisced, passing Courtney a bowl of steaming vegetables.

Tony groaned, covering his face with his hands. "I thought we agreed never to speak of that again!"

Courtney grinned, the memories vivid and cherished. "Oh, come on! It was a masterpiece...until your dad found us and made us clean it all up."

As the laughter and conversation continued, Courtney felt a warmth blossoming in her chest. This was what she had been missing in her fast-paced city life—the unconditional love and acceptance of family, the comfort of shared history, and the undeniable sense of belonging.

In that moment, surrounded by the people who had shaped her childhood and now welcomed her back with open arms, Courtney realized that sometimes, the path to true happiness led right back to where you started.

As the evening wore on, the gentle patter of raindrops began to echo against the farmhouse roof. The wind picked up, whistling through the screen door and carrying with it the earthy scent of impending rain. James glanced out the window, a smile playing at the corners of his mouth. "Looks like we're in for a good old-fashioned thunderstorm, folks."

Eileen bustled into the living room, a steaming

apple pie cradled in her oven mitt-clad hands. The sweet, cinnamon-laced aroma of baked apples wafted through the air.

"Nothing beats homemade pie on a stormy night," she declared as she set the golden-crusted dessert on the coffee table. "Tony, why don't you build us a fire in the hearth? It'll keep us cozy."

Tony nodded, already rolling up his sleeves. "On it, Mom." He shot Courtney a playful wink as he passed by, sending a flutter through her stomach.

As Tony knelt by the fireplace, arranging kindling and logs with practiced ease, Courtney found herself drawn to his side. She watched, mesmerized, as his strong hands coaxed a spark to life, nurturing it until flames danced merrily among the wood.

Straightening up, Tony turned to face her, the flickering firelight casting warm shadows across his features. "Remember when we used to roast marshmallows in here as kids?"

Courtney grinned, the memory vivid and sweet. "Of course! You always managed to set yours on fire, every single time."

He chuckled, rubbing the back of his neck. "What can I say? I like 'em crispy."

Their eyes met, and for a moment, the rest of the

world fell away. In the depths of Tony's gaze, Courtney saw a reflection of the emotions swirling within her own heart—affection, longing, and the promise of something more.

A particularly loud crack of thunder broke the spell, causing them both to jump. Laughter bubbled up as they settled onto the couch, the old springs creaking beneath them.

Eileen handed out plates heaped with generous slices of pie, the flaky crust glistening with a dusting of sugar. "Dig in, everyone! There's plenty more where that came from."

As Courtney savored the first bite, the flavors of tart apple and warm spices dancing on her tongue, she couldn't help but marvel at the perfection of the moment. The storm raged outside, but within the walls of the Turner farmhouse, all was warm, safe, and filled with love.

Tony's arm brushed against hers as he reached for his own plate, sending a tingle racing along her skin. In that instant, Courtney knew with startling clarity that this was where she belonged—not in some sleek city apartment, but here, surrounded by the people and places that had shaped her heart.

As the evening wore on, the storm gradually subsided, leaving behind a freshly-washed world glistening in the moonlight. Courtney and Tony found themselves lingering on the porch, reluctant to say goodnight.

Tony leaned against the railing, his eyes soft as he gazed at her. "It's really good to have you back, Court. Feels like old times, doesn't it?"

She smiled, her heart full to bursting. "It does." She placed her hand on Tony's arm as she said, "Thank you, Tony, for inviting me over. I didn't realize just how much I needed this."

Tony's cheeks colored, and he ducked his head bashfully as he said, "Anytime, Court. Anytime."

Chapter Seven

Courtney stood in her grandmother's kitchen, surrounded by the familiar scent of cinnamon and pine. Her long, dark hair was swept up in a hasty bun to keep it out of the way as she methodically laid out the ingredients for the special Christmas dinner she had planned. The old farmhouse hummed with the quiet anticipation of the holiday, and the soft glow from the strings of lights added a cozy warmth to the room. It was her way of saying thank you to Tony, the man who'd gone out of his way to make her feel at home again.

"Alright," Courtney murmured to herself, double-checking the recipe card in her grandmother's neat script. "Roast chicken, garlic mashed potatoes, green beans almondine, and...oh, what am I forgetting?"

The doorbell rang, slicing through her concentration. She wiped her hands on her apron and moved to the door, her heart skipping a beat. Opening it, she found Tony standing there with his signature easy smile and a basket filled with fresh produce from his farm.

"Tony! You're early," Courtney said, surprise coloring her tone as much as pleasure.

"Figured I could lend a hand, if that's alright with you," Tony replied, stepping in with the ease of a man who felt no need to stand on ceremony.

"I—well, sure, but you didn't have to..." Courtney began, her polished demeanor faltering before the genuine kindness in his eyes.

"Didn't have to, but wanted to," he interjected gently, setting the basket down on the counter. "Now, what's on the menu, ma'am?"

In the kitchen, Tony rolled up his sleeves, revealing forearms marked by the labor of farm life. They set to work side by side, and soon the room was alive with the sounds of chopping and sizzling, punctuated by laughter. Tony proved to be surprisingly adept with a knife, though his technique was more about enthusiasm than finesse.

"Watch your fingers, Tony, or we'll be serving roast chicken with a side of Band-Aids," Courtney teased, as he narrowly missed nicking himself while dicing carrots.

"Ah, just adding a little excitement to the process," Tony quipped, grinning as he brandished the knife with exaggerated caution.

"Excitement is not an ingredient I'm familiar with," she retorted playfully, shaking her head.

Courtney watched as Tony reached into the fridge and somehow managed to knock over a carton of eggs with his elbow. A few made a mad dash for freedom, only to meet their end on the tile floor.

"Oops." His sheepish grin was infectious, and Courtney couldn't help but laugh as she grabbed some paper towels.

"Your egg-juggling act needs work," she said, bending to clean up the mess.

"Guess I'm better with chickens when they're above ground," Tony admitted with a chuckle, helping her wipe up the evidence of his culinary mishap.

As they prepared the meal together, their movements around the kitchen became a comfortable dance. The atmosphere was charged with an energy that was part festive and part something more—a connection that seemed to grow stronger with each shared smile and brush of the hand.

"Okay, Mr. Turner, time to tackle the mashed potatoes," Courtney announced, pointing to the pot of peeled potatoes waiting on the countertop.

"Ma'am, yes ma'am!" Tony saluted mockingly and then took charge of mashing them with a vigor that left Courtney both amused and slightly concerned for the integrity of the pot.

"Easy, Tony. We're making dinner, not digging a new well," she laughed, her voice warm and light.

"Can't help it," he said with a wide, boyish grin. "I've got all this farming strength and nowhere to put it."

"Clearly," she responded, giving him a playful nudge with her hip as she reached for the butter.

"Besides," he continued, his drawl wrapping around the words like a gentle hug, "I aim to make these the best darn mashed potatoes you ever tasted."

Courtney looked over at Tony, his face alight with merriment, and felt a swell of gratitude. He was right there, in her grandmother's kitchen, bringing joy into a place she'd once thought would forever be tinged with sadness.

"Hey, Tony, can you grab this?"

Courtney asked as she reached for a box perched

precariously atop the fridge. Her voice carried a hint of excitement mixed with reverence. She'd been meaning to pull the dusty box down for a few days now.

"Sure thing," Tony replied, sidestepping her to reach the box. As he set it down on the kitchen table, a soft jingle echoed from within, like a whisper from Christmases past.

Courtney's fingers danced over the cardboard flaps, freeing them one by one. She carefully lifted out layers of tissue paper, revealing delicate treasures beneath. Then, nestled between a pair of glass angels, she found it—a beautifully crafted sewn ornament, its surface a tapestry of vibrant colors and intricate patterns.

"Grandmother made this," she breathed, cradling the ornament in her palm. The light caught in the facets of the glass ornaments still in the box, sending prisms dancing across her face. "She was so talented..."

"Looks like it took a lot of love to make that," Tony observed, leaning in to admire the handiwork. His eyes softened, reflecting the glow of the Christmas lights strung around the room.

"More than you know." Courtney's smile was tinged with nostalgia as she held the ornament up to the light. "She used to say that every stitch was a prayer for our family."

"Then it's more than just beautiful, it's blessed." Tony's voice was gentle, and it wrapped around Courtney like a warm blanket.

"Exactly," she whispered, feeling an unexpected surge of connection to her roots. "Honestly, these were always the best Christmas gifts, knowing that she handmade them herself."

Before the moment could stretch too long, Tony cleared his throat and reached into his pocket. "Speaking of gifts," he began, "I have something for you, too."

He produced a small, hand-carved wooden figure—a replica of Courtney's childhood home, complete with tiny windows and a miniature front porch. Courtney gasped, her hands flying to her mouth as tears brimmed in her eyes.

"Tony, this is...it's this house! How did you—?"

"Spent some evenings whittling away in the workshop," he admitted, his cheeks tinged with pink. "Wanted to give you a piece of home you could take with you wherever you go."

"Thank you," she said, her voice barely above a whisper. She touched the little chimney, memories flooding back of smoke curling up into winter skies and laughter echoing through halls.

"Seems fitting," Tony said. "You've brought so much warmth back to this place, just like that house was always full of love."

"Your hands crafted this?" Courtney marveled, tracing the lines of the tiny shingles. "It's exquisite."

"Only the best for you," he declared with a playful wink. "And hey, if you shake it, there's a surprise."

Curious, Courtney gave the little house a gentle shake and watched in delight as snowflakes began to swirl inside the clear base. "It's a snow globe, too!" she exclaimed. "Tony, I can't believe you made this."

"Believe it," he said with a chuckle. "And every time you see it, remember that no matter how far you go, there's always love waiting for you here."

Courtney hung the precious gift on the Christmas tree beside her grandmother's ornament, a symbol of the new memories forged alongside the old. The room seemed to glow with an even warmer light as they shared smiles that spoke volumes beyond words.

Courtney watched the snowflakes dance in the globe, a soft lullaby of winter's touch encapsulated in glass. The pine-scented candles flickered nearby, casting a warm glow over the room, wrapping it—and them—in Christmas magic. From the kitchen, the aromas of their dinner mingled together, an olfactory symphony that promised more than just a festive feast.

"Looks like we're all set," Tony said as he carried the platter to the table, his eyes never leaving hers.

"Almost," she replied, standing to help him adjust the spread, their hands brushing over the embroidered tablecloth her grandmother had once made. Every stitch told a story, every patch a memory, and now Tony's presence wove new threads into the fabric of her life.

"Perfect," he declared with that signature grin that always seemed to light up the room. His gaze lingered on her for a moment longer than necessary, making her heart do an awkward little two-step.

"Would you do the honors?" Courtney asked, handing him the ornate carving knife and fork set that had been used for so many family gatherings. It felt right, passing it to him, as if he were already part of something bigger than just tonight's dinner.

"Only if you promise to save me some of that pecan pie you've been bragging about," Tony teased, accepting the utensils.

"Deal," she laughed, feeling a warmth that had

nothing to do with the oven or the candles. It was something deeper, a glow from within that she hadn't felt in years.

As they settled into their seats, Courtney couldn't help but notice how easily Tony fit into this scene, as if he'd always been there. He said grace with a sincerity that made her close her eyes and really listen, not just to his words, but to the unspoken messages between them.

"Thank you for this food, for friends who are like family, and for the blessings of this season," Tony finished, squeezing her hand gently before releasing it.

"Amen," Courtney echoed, her voice softer than she intended. As they began to eat, laughter and stories flowed between them as naturally as the wine in their glasses. She found herself watching him, the way he savored each bite, the crinkles at the corners of his eyes when he smiled, the genuine interest with which he listened to her recount tales of city life.

"Sounds like you're living the dream out there," Tony observed, passing her the bowl of green beans.

"Sometimes," she admitted, twirling her fork. "But dreams change, don't they?"

"Suppose they do," he mused. "Sometimes what you need has been right in front of you all along."

Her heart skipped again, betraying her cool exterior. Was he talking about the farm, the town, or something else entirely? The candlelight danced in his eyes, reflecting a hope she dared not name—not yet.

"Tony, I..." She paused, searching for the right words. "I can't thank you enough for being here, for everything."

"Wouldn't be anywhere else," he assured her, reaching across the table to give her hand another gentle squeeze. This time, she held on, allowing the contact to linger.

In that moment, as the soft strains of "O Come All Ye Faithful" played in the background and the world outside hushed under a blanket of snow, Courtney realized that her carefully constructed walls were crumbling. Piece by piece, Tony Turner was rebuilding them into something new—a home not just of brick and mortar, but of love and laughter.

And as the evening wore on, with the crackle of the fireplace mixing with the melodies of Christmas and the comfort of shared silence, Courtney knew without a doubt that she was slowly, irrevocably, falling in love with Tony Turner.

Chapter Eight

Courtney sat at her grandmother's old oak desk, the worn leather journal open before her. The yellowed pages were filled with her grandmother's elegant script, detailing acts of kindness and community spirit from decades past. A sudden idea struck Courtney, and she reached for her phone.

"Tony, it's Courtney. I was just reading through my grandmother's journal and I had an idea. What if we organized a charity drive to help those in need right here in our community? We could collect food, clothes, toys for the kids. Really make a difference this holiday season."

There was a brief pause on the other end of the

line. "That's a mighty fine idea, Courtney. Your grandmother, she always had a way of bringing out the best in folks. I reckon this town could use some of that spirit right about now."

Courtney smiled, picturing the twinkle in Tony's eye. "Great! Let's meet up tomorrow and start making plans. I'll bring coffee and donuts."

"You sure do know the way to a man's heart," Tony chuckled. "I'll see you bright and early."

The next morning, they huddled together at a corner table in the local diner, sipping steaming mugs of coffee as they scribbled notes and brainstormed ideas. Tony's face lit up as he described the families he knew who could benefit from their efforts.

"I was thinking," Courtney said, leaning in closer, "we could make flyers to hang up around town. Maybe even reach out to the local radio station for a spot on the morning show."

Tony nodded enthusiastically. "That's a great idea. I can talk to some of the other farmers, see if they'd be willing to pitch in some fresh produce for the food baskets."

As they worked, their hands brushed against each other, sending a tingle up Courtney's arm. She glanced up, catching Tony's warm gaze.

The shared a smile that set Courtney's heart fluttering, and she realized she was happier than she could remember being in a long time.

Over the next few days, they threw themselves into promoting the drive. Courtney designed eyecatching flyers, while Tony spread the word among his friends and neighbors. Together, they manned a donation booth in the town square, greeting passersby with bright smiles and genuine enthusiasm.

As the donations poured in—cans of food, gently used coats, shiny new toys—Courtney felt a swell of pride. This was what her grandmother had always talked about, the power of community coming together to lift each other up.

She turned to Tony, who was helping an elderly woman carry her bags of donations to the booth. The caring, easy way he interacted with everyone who crossed his path made Courtney's heart flutter. She realized that through this partnership, she was not only reconnecting with her roots and honoring her grandmother's legacy, but also forging a deep and meaningful bond with a truly special man.

As they sorted through the latest batch of donations, Courtney held up a plush toy cow with a quizzical expression. "Hey Tony, what do you think about cows? They seem like pretty great animals, don't they?"

Tony chuckled, his eyes crinkling at the corners. "Cows are alright, I suppose. But have you ever really looked at a pig? Those fellas are the real MVPs of the farm, if you ask me."

Courtney raised an eyebrow, a playful smirk on her lips. "Oh really? Do tell, Mr. Turner. What makes pigs so special?"

"Well, for starters, they're smart as a whip. Did you know pigs can solve puzzles and play video games? They've got a real knack for problem-solving." Tony leaned against the donation table, a mischievous glint in his eye.

"Video games? Come on, Tony. Now you're just pulling my leg!" Courtney laughed, shaking her head in disbelief.

"I'm serious! Researchers have done studies on it and everything. Plus, pigs are social creatures. They form strong bonds with each other and even with their human caretakers. Kinda like dogs, but with a snout and a curly tail."

Courtney considered this for a moment, absently

fiddling with the toy cow's soft ears. "I guess I never really thought about pigs that way. But you know what animal I think is underrated? Sheep! They're so fluffy and cute, and they provide us with wool for cozy sweaters and blankets."

"Sheep are mighty fine, I'll give you that. But have you ever tried to herd a flock of 'em? It's like trying to corral a bunch of toddlers hopped up on sugar. Give me a pig any day!" Tony grinned, his laughter ringing out across the town square.

Courtney couldn't help but join in, her shoulders shaking with mirth. "Okay, okay, I concede. Pigs are pretty great. But I still think cows are the most huggable."

"Well, I don't know about huggable, but they sure do make a mean burger!" Tony winked, eliciting another round of laughter from Courtney.

As their laughter subsided, Courtney marveled at the easy banter they shared. Even in the midst of their hard work and dedication to the charity drive, Tony always found a way to make her smile and forget her worries. She realized that this connection they had forged—built on shared values, laughter, and a deep appreciation for the simple things in life —was truly something special.

With a contented sigh, Courtney turned back to

the donation boxes, a renewed sense of purpose and joy in her heart. Side by side with Tony, she knew they could face any challenge that came their way—one silly farm animal debate at a time.

The day of the deliveries arrived, crisp and clear, with a hint of wood smoke in the air. Courtney and Tony loaded up his pickup truck with the fruits of their labor—boxes overflowing with food, gifts, and essentials. They set off down the winding country roads, a map of local families in need guiding their way.

Their first stop was a small, tidy house at the edge of town. A young mother answered the door, a baby balanced on her hip. Her eyes widened as Courtney and Tony unloaded a box filled with diapers, formula, and warm winter clothes.

"I don't know how to thank you," the woman said, her voice trembling with emotion. "This means more than you could ever know."

Courtney felt a lump form in her throat. "We're just happy to help," she managed, her hand finding Tony's and giving it a grateful squeeze.

As they drove to the next house, Courtney

watched the countryside roll by, lost in thought. She had always been proud of her corporate success, but this—making a real, tangible difference in people's lives—felt like a different kind of accomplishment altogether.

Tony seemed to sense her contemplation. "Penny for your thoughts?" he asked, glancing over with a gentle smile.

Courtney sighed, trying to put her feelings into words. "It's just...I never realized how good it could feel to help people like this. To see the direct impact of your actions."

Tony nodded, his eyes soft with understanding. "That's what community is all about, isn't it? Looking out for each other, lifting each other up. It's how I was raised, and it's what I've always tried to do."

Courtney felt a rush of affection for this kind, steadfast man beside her. "You're really good at it, you know," she said softly. "Helping people. Making them feel seen and cared for."

Tony ducked his head, a bashful smile playing at his lips. "Well, I could say the same about you, Miss Big City Marketing Exec. You've got a heart of gold under that power suit."

Courtney laughed, the sound mingling with the rustling of the wind through the bare trees. For the first time in a long time, she felt truly at peace—with herself, with her path, and with the man by her side who made it all feel right.

Chapter Nine

Courtney's cell phone buzzed on her desk, a New York number flashing on the screen. She hesitated a moment before answering. "Hello, this is Courtney Rivera."

"Courtney, hi! It's Steve Larson from Halcyon Marketing. I have some exciting news. We've reviewed your file, and we'd like to offer you the Vice President of Marketing position. Your experience and skills are exactly what we need to take our campaigns to the next level. The salary and benefits package are very competitive. In fact, I'll go so far as to say I don't think you'll find a better offer in the Big Apple." He chuckled.

Courtney's grip tightened on the phone as a mix

of emotions swirled inside her. The prestige, the paycheck, the thrill of climbing the corporate ladder once again all beckoned to her like a siren song.

"Wow Steve, I'm flattered by the offer. Can I take a day or two to think it over and discuss with my family? It would be a big move."

"Of course, I understand. But don't wait too long—an opportunity like this doesn't come around often! I look forward to hearing back from you soon."

Courtney thanked him and hung up the phone, her mind reeling. She walked over to the window, hugging her arms around herself as she gazed out at the rustic charm of her hometown. The twinkling Christmas lights, the merry wreaths on lampposts, the neighborly smiles and waves as people passed by.

Of course, she was only here through Christmas. The plan was always that she would go back to the city and resume her life.

Right?

Unbidden, childhood memories of baking cookies with Grandma, sledding with her old friends, and caroling with the Turners surfaced, tugging at her heartstrings.

But then the gleaming skyscrapers and bustling

streets of New York beckoned too, reminding her of the thrills and challenges that made her feel so alive.

Torn between two paths, Courtney did the only thing she could think of—she prayed. Bowing her head, she poured out her conflicted heart to God.

"Lord, I don't know what to do. New York holds so much promise for my career, but Kentucky...this is my home. These people... Please guide me to make the right choice..."

She held still for a long moment, hoping for a clear sign or answer. But there was nothing.

She didn't feel the familiar peace that often washed over her when she prayed.

She frowned and opened her eyes. With a gentle exhale of frustration, she rose from her chair and headed out for a walk in the brisk winter air, hoping the holiday beauty around her would spark some clarity as to where her heart truly belonged.

Eventually, her feet led her to the local diner, where she saw Tony.

He instantly motioned her over to his booth.

She slid across from him, but Tony's warm smile faded when he noticed the pensive expression on Courtney's face.

"What's on your mind, Courtney?" he asked gently, reaching across the table to take her hand.

Courtney sighed, fiddling with the menu. "I got a job offer in New York. A big promotion actually."

Tony's eyes widened, a flicker of surprise and something else—disappointment, perhaps?—crossing his features. "Wow, that's...that's great news. Congratulations," he said, his voice measured.

"Thanks," Courtney replied, searching his face. "I haven't decided if I'm going to take it yet."

Tony nodded slowly, his gaze dropping to the table. "It's a fantastic opportunity. You'd be crazy not to go for it," he said quietly, though his words lacked conviction.

An awkward silence settled between them, heavy with unspoken emotions. Courtney's heart ached at the thought of leaving Tony, of walking away from the special connection they'd forged. But the allure of her career, of proving herself in the cutthroat corporate world, tugged at her too.

Though they tried to act normal, the usual comfort and joviality they'd shared the past couple weeks was absent as they both ate their food quietly, making small talk here and there like stilted strangers.

Courtney's heart ached.

That night, Courtney tossed and turned in her grandmother's old bed, the worn quilt tangled around her legs. Sleep eluded her as her mind raced with the weight of her decision.

New York meant success, wealth, the thrill of climbing the corporate ladder. It meant fancy parties, designer clothes, and a life of luxury. But it also meant long hours, high stress, and a constant pressure to prove herself.

Kentucky, on the other hand, offered a different kind of richness. The warmth of community, the joy of simple pleasures, the chance to put down roots in a place that felt like home. Here, she had Tony, a man who made her heart skip and her soul feel at peace.

Of course, they hadn't pledged themselves to each other or anything. Courtney blushed at her assumptive thoughts and forced herself to abandon that line of thinking.

Tony aside, she was really starting to feel at home here again.

Courtney sighed, rolling onto her back to stare at the ceiling. The old house creaked and groaned around her, as if sharing its own opinion on the matter. Could she really start over here, in this sleepy little town? Could she be content with a life so different from the one she'd always imagined?

As the night wore on, Courtney's thoughts chased each other in circles, offering no clear answers. She knew she had to make a choice—and soon. But for now, all she could do was pray for guidance and trust that, in the end, God would lead her down the right path.

Chapter Ten

Tony stood on Courtney's front porch, his heart pounding beneath his flannel shirt. Snow flurries danced in the crisp night air, catching in his dark hair. He clutched a worn envelope in his rough hands, the paper soft from years tucked away. He took a deep breath and knocked on her door.

Courtney opened it, surprise flashing across her elegant features. "Tony! What are you doing here? Is everything okay?" Her eyes, fringed by long lashes, shone with concern.

"I...uh...I have something for you," he stammered, thrusting the letter towards her. As her slender fingers closed around it, he rambled on, "I wrote this a long time ago, back when we were kids. I wasn't sure about giving it to you, but...well, I know you've got this whole life in the city now, and that's great, it really is, but I just couldn't let you leave again without telling you..."

His voice trailed off as Courtney unfolded the letter, her eyes skimming the childish scrawl. He watched, scarcely breathing, as a glimmer of tears welled up in her eyes. She looked back at him, and he felt his heart constrict. *Lord, she was beautiful, just like always.*

"Tony..." She whispered his name like a prayer.

"I love you, Courtney," he blurted out, the words tumbling free. "I always have, ever since we were kids running 'round these hills. And I know I ain't got much to offer, just this farm and my heart, but..." His voice cracked, thick with emotion. "I want a life with you. I can't leave, not with Ma and Pa counting on me, but I'm asking you to stay. Here, with me."

Courtney gazed at him, a whirlwind of emotions playing across her face. The letter trembled in her hands. Tony held his breath, hope and fear battling in his chest. This was it, the moment of truth. He'd laid his heart bare, and now all he could do was pray she felt the same. He reached out, gently taking her hand in his. "Please, Courtney..."

Courtney's heart swelled as she gazed into Tony's earnest eyes, his rough hand enveloping hers with a tender warmth that felt like home. In that moment, the bustling city life she'd built seemed to fade away, replaced by a profound sense of belonging right here, in the rolling hills of Kentucky, with the man who had always held her heart.

"Oh, Tony," she breathed, a tearful smile breaking across her face. "I've been so blind, chasing after a dream I thought I wanted, when everything I ever needed was right here all along."

She stepped closer, the letter fluttering to the ground as she reached up to cradle his face in her hands. "I love you too, Tony Turner. I always have, and I always will."

Tony's eyes widened, a disbelieving joy spreading across his features. "You mean it? You'll stay?"

Courtney nodded, laughing softly as happy tears spilled down her cheeks. "Yes, I'll stay. This is where I belong, here with you."

Unable to contain the love bursting within him, Tony swept her into his arms, spinning her around as they both laughed with pure, unbridled joy. As he set her down, their eyes locked, a magnetic pull drawing them closer until their lips met in a kiss that held the promise of a lifetime.

In that perfect moment, as the winter sun dipped below the horizon and the twinkling lights of the farmhouse cast a warm glow across the snow-dusted landscape, Courtney and Tony sealed their commitment to each other, their hearts intertwined in a love that had finally found its way home.

Chapter Eleven

A gentle knock roused Courtney from her slumber. She blinked her eyes open, momentarily disoriented, then remembered—it was Christmas morning in her grandmother's house—well, *her* house now—in Kentucky. Stretching, she padded over to the door and smiled when she saw Tony standing there.

He immediately wrapped her in a hug. "Merry Christmas, sleephead," he told her as he dropped a kiss on her forehead.

"Merry Christmas." She squeezed him back. "Let me throw on some clothes, and I'll be ready."

Tony sat in the oversized chair her grandma used to sit in and waited patiently while Courtney returned to her bedroom to get dressed for Christmas morning breakfast with the Turners.

Tony handed Courtney a thermos of coffee sweetened just the way she liked it as she got in his old pickup truck. Her heart swelled. "You know me so well," she commented.

He winked at her. "You know it."

Courtney took in the pristine blanket of snow that glistened in the early morning light as Tony's truck ambled down the road toward his family's farms. She couldn't help but marvel at how beautiful it all looked as it covered the fields and barns. It was like a fresh start, full of promise and possibility.

Just like her budding relationship with Tony, Courtney thought with a smile. This magical scene felt like a sign of the new beginnings ahead of them.

Tony held the door open for her, and savory aromas of frying bacon and brewing coffee filled the cozy space. A fire crackled merrily in the hearth.

"Well, look what the cat dragged in," Mr. Turner teased as Tony and Courtney stepped through the doorway.

"Merry Christmas," Courtney replied with a laugh. "Everything smells amazing, Mrs. Turner."

"Merry Christmas, sweetheart." Tony's mother engulfed Courtney in a warm hug. "We're so happy you could join us, dear. Come, sit! Breakfast is ready."

As they gathered around the table piled high with breakfast delights, easy chatter and laughter filled the air. Mr. Turner said grace, his head bowed and weathered hands clasped, thanking the Lord for their many blessings—especially for bringing Courtney home.

Courtney felt tears prick her eyes, overcome with gratitude to be included in their family traditions. In New York, Christmas had been a subdued affair—just her alone watching Christmas movies. But here, enveloped by the Turners' love and Tony's steady presence at her side, her heart swelled with a profound sense of belonging.

Under the table, Tony reached for her hand and squeezed. He leaned in close. "Having you here...it's the best Christmas gift I could ask for."

"Me too," Courtney whispered. For the first time in a long time, she felt truly at home, at peace. Like she was exactly where she was meant to be.

After they cleared the table and gathered to sit in front of the fireplace in the living room, Tony cleared his throat, drawing the attention of his parents. He stood and took Courtney's hand. She looked up at him quizzically, her heart fluttering in anticipation.

"Mom, Dad," Tony began, his voice thick with emotion. "Having Courtney here with us today has made me realize just how much I want her to be a part of our family. Not just today, but every day, for the rest of our lives."

He turned to Courtney, his blue eyes shining with love and tenderness. Slowly, he lowered himself to one knee, reaching into his pocket to retrieve a small velvet box.

Courtney gasped, her hands flying to her mouth as tears welled in her eyes.

"Courtney Rivera," Tony said, his voice steady and sure, "you know I've loved you since we were kids. I should have never let you get away all those years ago. I can't imagine spending another day without you by my side."

He opened the box, revealing a simple yet stunning diamond ring. "Will you marry me?"

Tears streaming down her face, Courtney nodded. "Yes," she whispered, her voice choked with emotion. "Yes, Tony, I will marry you."

Tony's parents erupted in joyous cheers as he slipped the ring onto Courtney's finger, then swept her into his arms for a chaste kiss and hug. Mrs. Turner wept happily, clutching her husband's arm, while Mr. Turner beamed with pride, clapping his son on the back.

"Welcome to the family, Courtney," he said warmly, enveloping her in a hug. "Well, you've always been a part of our family, but you know what I mean." He winked at her, looking so much like Tony as he did so that Courtney's heart swelled further.

Courtney clung to Tony, her heart overflowing with love and gratitude. She had found her home, her family, her forever.

Later that day, as the sun began to set, Courtney and Tony walked hand-in-hand through the snow-covered cemetery. They stopped before a simple headstone, and Courtney knelt, brushing away the snow to reveal her grandmother's name.

"Hi, Grandma," she whispered, her breath forming small clouds in the chilly air. "I wanted to tell you...I'm getting married. To Tony." Her lips tipped up into a smile. "That probably comes as no surprise to you."

Tony placed a comforting hand on her shoulder,

and Courtney leaned into his touch, drawing strength from his presence.

"I miss you so much," she continued, her voice trembling. "But I know you're watching over me. And I know that you're happy for me. For us."

She placed a single white lily on the grave—her grandma's favorite flower—then stood, turning to face Tony. He wrapped his arms around her, holding her close as she let the tears fall.

"She's always with you," he murmured, pressing a gentle kiss to her temple. "And so am I. Forever and always."

Courtney smiled through her tears, secure in the knowledge that her grandmother would have approved.

When they pulled apart, Tony took her hand and they began to walk quietly.

As they walked through the picturesque countryside, the snow crunched beneath their feet, leaving a trail of footprints behind them. The sun peeked through the clouds, casting a soft, golden glow over the pristine landscape. Courtney breathed in the crisp, winter air, feeling a sense of peace and contentment wash over her.

Tony squeezed her hand, drawing her attention.

"Penny for your thoughts?" he asked, his blue eyes twinkling with affection.

Courtney smiled, her heart swelling with love for the man beside her. "I was just thinking about how perfect this moment is. How lucky I am to have you in my life."

"I'm the lucky one," Tony replied, pulling her closer. "You've brought so much joy and light into my world, Courtney. I can't imagine spending my life with anyone else."

They paused at the top of a small hill, taking in the breathtaking view of the snow-covered fields and the distant mountains. The world seemed to stretch out before them, full of promise and potential.

"I love you, Tony," Courtney said, her voice soft but filled with conviction. "I can't wait to start our life together, to build a future with you."

"I love you too, Courtney," Tony replied, his voice thick with emotion. "More than words can express. You're my everything."

They sealed their declaration with a tender kiss, their hearts beating as one. As they broke apart, Courtney rested her head on Tony's shoulder, content to simply be in his presence.

Together, they continued their walk, their laughter

echoing through the tranquil countryside. The future stretched out before them, bright and full of hope. They knew that with their love and God to guide them, they could face anything that life threw their way.

And as the sun began to set, painting the sky in hues of pink and orange, Courtney and Tony made their way back home to his farm, ready to start their happily ever after.

CHRISTMAS IN VIRGINIA

Lauren's car rolled to a stop at the familiar intersection, the old traffic light swaying gently in the crisp December breeze. Her eyes lingered on the faded "Welcome to Oakridge" sign, its peeling paint a testament to the passage of time. A smile tugged at her lips as she breathed in the scent of pine and woodsmoke that wafted through her cracked window.

"Home sweet home," she murmured, her fingers drumming a soft rhythm on the steering wheel.

As the light turned green, Lauren eased her foot off the brake, allowing her car to glide down Main Street. The storefronts, decked out in twinkling lights and garlands, beckoned to her like old friends. She couldn't help but chuckle at the sight of Mr.

Thompson's hardware store, its windows still plastered with the same faded posters she remembered from childhood.

Some things never change, she thought, a warmth spreading through her chest.

Her gaze drifted to the old oak tree in the town square, its bare branches now adorned with hundreds of colorful ornaments. Memories flooded back—of hot cocoa sipped while decorating the tree with her parents, of carols sung off-key but with heart, of laughter shared with friends and neighbors.

Lauren slowed the car, allowing herself to drink in the sight of the elaborate Christmas display outside the school. "Oh, Mama would love to see this," she said aloud, making a mental note to bring her parents here later.

As she turned onto Maple Avenue, the scent of freshly baked gingerbread wafted through the air, transporting her back to countless Christmas Eves spent in her mother's kitchen. Lauren's stomach growled in response, and she smiled.

The familiar houses lining the street tugged at her heartstrings. Each one held a story, a memory. There was the Johnsons' place, where she and her best friend Mary had built countless snowmen. And the Wilsons' house, with its grand porch where they'd held impromptu caroling sessions.

Lauren's chest tightened with a bittersweet ache. *I've missed this so much*, she thought. *Why did I stay away for so long?*

As she approached her childhood home, Lauren felt a mix of excitement and nervousness bubbling up inside her. The house looked just as she remembered—the wreath on the door, the soft glow of candlelight in the windows, the smoke curling from the chimney.

Well, here goes nothing. Lauren took a deep breath as she pulled into the driveway. *Time to face the music—and Mama's infamous interrogations about my love life.*

With a gentle laugh, she stepped out of the car, the crunch of snow beneath her boots a welcome sound. The porch light flickered on, and Lauren's heart swelled with love and anticipation.

"Home," she breathed, "I'm finally home."

Lauren stepped onto the porch, her heart racing as she raised her hand to knock. Before her knuckles could touch the wood, the door swung open, revealing her mother's beaming face.

"Lauren, sweetheart!" her mother exclaimed,

pulling her into a warm embrace. "Oh, how we've missed you!"

The scent of cinnamon enveloped Lauren as she hugged her mother back. "I've missed you too, Mama," she said, her voice muffled against her mother's shoulder.

As they pulled apart, Lauren's father appeared behind her mother, his eyes twinkling. "There's our city girl," he said with a chuckle. "Come on in before you freeze out there."

Lauren stepped inside, the warmth of the house washing over her. The living room was adorned with twinkling lights and garlands, the Christmas tree standing proud in the corner. Memories flooded back, bringing a lump to her throat.

"It's perfect," she whispered, taking it all in. "Just like I remember."

Her mother squeezed her hand. "We've been waiting all day to hear about your big city adventures. How's that fancy marketing job treating you?"

Lauren's smile faltered slightly. "It's...challenging," she admitted, sinking onto the familiar plush sofa. "Sometimes I wonder if I made the right choice, moving away."

Her father settled into his armchair, leaning

forward. "Now, now, pumpkin. Remember what we always say in this family?"

Lauren couldn't help but grin. "God has a plan for everything," they recited in unison, laughing.

As the evening wore on, they shared stories and laughter, the warmth of family wrapping around Lauren like a cozy blanket. She found herself relaxing, the stress of city life melting away.

It was good to be home.

The next morning, Lauren decided to grab breakfast at Milly's Diner, a local favorite. As she settled into a booth, the aroma of fresh coffee and syrupy pancakes filled the air.

"Well, if it isn't Lauren Beard!" Milly herself called out, bustling over with a pot of coffee. "Home for the holidays, sugar?"

Lauren nodded, smiling. "Yep."

As Milly poured her coffee, Lauren couldn't help but overhear the conversation from the next booth.

"Did you hear about that new fella in town?" a familiar voice gossiped. "Shane something-or-other. Moved into old Mrs. Peterson's place."

Lauren's ears perked up, her curiosity piqued despite herself.

"Oh, I saw him at the grocery store," another voice chimed in. "Handsome as can be, but awfully quiet. Wonder what his story is?"

Lauren sipped her coffee, her mind whirling with questions about this mysterious newcomer. She caught herself and shook her head, chuckling softly. Some things really didn't change—small town gossip was alive and well.

But who was she to talk? She was here all of one day and she was already feeding into it too.

She stirred her coffee absently, her mind still buzzing with thoughts of the enigmatic Shane Fisher. The chatter of the diner faded into background noise as she found herself lost in contemplation.

"Penny for your thoughts?" Milly's voice cut through her reverie.

Lauren looked up, a sheepish smile playing on her lips. "Oh, just...thinking about how some things never change around here."

Milly chuckled, refilling Lauren's cup. "Like our fondness for a good mystery, you mean?"

"Exactly," Lauren replied, her eyes twinkling. "So, what's your take on this Shane character?"

Milly leaned in conspiratorially. "Well, he's been coming in for breakfast most mornings. Always orders the same thing—black coffee and wheat toast. Scribbles in this tattered old journal of his."

Lauren's marketing instincts kicked in. "A writer, maybe?"

"Could be," Milly nodded. "Though what brings a writer to our little town is beyond me."

Lauren's gaze drifted to the frost-covered window, watching as early morning shoppers bustled along the sidewalk. "Maybe he's looking for inspiration," she mused, more to herself than to Milly.

As she turned back, Lauren caught sight of a tall figure entering the diner. His disheveled dark hair was dusted with snowflakes, and he carried himself with a quiet confidence that immediately drew her attention.

"Well, speak of the devil," Milly whispered, straightening up. "That's him now."

Lauren's heart skipped a beat as she watched Shane Fisher make his way to the counter, his piercing blue eyes scanning the room briefly before settling on an empty stool. She found herself wondering what stories those eyes held, what had brought him to this small corner of Virginia.

And that's when he looked up and his eyes met hers.

Lauren couldn't quite stop her gasp. He stared at her so intently, it was like he was looking right through her.

Her face colored and she looked back down at her coffee, her heart thumping.

When she finally got the courage to look back up, he was gone.

Shane something-or-other was a mystery indeed.

About the Author

Award-winning author Kayla Lowe writes women's fiction that explores complex themes with sensitivity and depth. Kayla's books delve into the intricacies of relationships, self-discovery, and resilience. From cozy love stories interspersed with a bit of faith to heartwarming tales of friendship and suspenseful novels of empowerment and heartbreak, her books illustrate the struggles specific to women.

When she's not churning out her next novel, you can find her with her feet in the sand and a book in her hand or curled up on the couch with her dogs.

Visit her website at www.authorkaylalowe.com.

Also by Kayla Lowe

Series

Christmas Blessings

Christmas Miracle for Two

A Christmas Promise of Love

A Christmas of Renewed Faith

Women of the Bible Fiction

Ruth

Esther

Rachel

Hannah

Deborah

Charms of the Chaste Court

A Courtship in Covent Garden

Whispers in Westminster

Romance in Regent's Park

Serenade on Strand Street

Treasure in Tower Bridge

Sweet Honey by the Sea

The Beekeeper's Secret (Book 1)

A Royal Honeycomb (Book 2)

Bees in Blossom (Book 3)

Honeyed Kisses (Book 4)

Blooming Forever (Book 5)

Strawberry Beach Series

Beachside Lessons (Book 1)

Beachside Lessons (Book 2)

Beachside Lessons (Book 3)

Panama City Beach Series

Sun-Kissed Secrets (Book 1)

Sun-Kissed Secrets (Book 2)

Sun-Kissed Secrets (Book 3)

The Tainted Love Saga

Of Love and Deception (Book 1)

Of Love and Family (Book 2)

Of Love and Violence (Book 3)

Of Love and Abuse(Book 4)

Of Love and Crime (Book 5)

Of Love and Addiction (Book 6)

Of Love and Redemption (Book 7)

Standalones

Maiden's Blush

Poetry

Phantom Poetry

Lost and Found